Enchanted:
Time and the Mountain

Jerilyn McIntyre

Illustrations by Ken Shuey

Bristlecone Peak * Interlaken, Utah

Related Works by the Author

Paws in the Piazza
Passi Felpati e Felini Alati
(with Grazia Adami Lovi)
The Shadow of the Unscratchable
Furball: A Harley T Katt Adventure
Harley Finds His Voice
Paws at Odds

ENCHANTED:
TIME and the MOUNTAIN

by Jerilyn McIntyre

2022

Bristlecone Peak Books
Interlaken, Utah

bristleconepeak.org
Printed in the United States of America

Library of Congress Control Number:
2022943081

ISBN:
978-0-9893753-9-9

Printed on acid-free paper

In memory of Joan Coles

THANK YOU

To Ken Shuey, the talented artist whose illustrations have captured the characters and the magical settings of *Enchanted*; to members of my writing group (Joan Coles, Klancy de Nevers, Donna Graves, Karen Hayes, Debbie Leaman, and Elizabeth Mitchell) for their thoughtful comments and suggestions on various earlier drafts of the manuscript; and to David Smith, business partner and spouse, for applying his considerable skills as an editor and designer to the publication of this book. A special acknowledgement to the memory of my parents, Maxine and Frank McIntyre, for introducing me to the wonder of storytelling; and a loving tribute to my late brother Joel, who in many respects in my life was the original version of Annie's brother Will.

Contents

THE BEAST AND THE FOREST

The creature trots the steep mountain ridge, looking along both sides, his eyes narrowed. Wind ruffles and spikes his fur and gusts across the rugged crest. He stops past the peak, points his snout toward the sky and howls, a long wail collapsing in a growl. This is his pathway. There are so many others. He scans, head low, then returns to the woods beneath the summit.

Down the slope, beyond the border of the tree line and deep in the dense forest, the aspen, fir, oak and pines sway, discordant, their branches and leaves whipping and rustling. Beneath their canopy, other animals hunker and shelter from the blustery weather. This wolf-like creature alone defies the harsh conditions. He stays on the prowl, old and alone. He is lord of the mountain, caretaker of all that is there, and this is his space.

L IFE in the forest is hard. Others—wolves, cougars and coyotes—prowl in search of prey. Deer, squirrels, chipmunks and different rodent-sized species feed in turn on different forms of life on the forest floor. From above, hawks and eagles sometimes swoop, patrolling their portion of the territory. Competition is fierce. And yet there is also cooperation and coexistence. Trees band together for nourishment. Their networks of roots and moss knit the underground plant world together. They lean on each other in heavy winds.

On this mountain, there is something more. Ancient and enduring, another reality, born of variations in the flow of time, has taken hold, higher and stronger than nature alone. The forest and its creatures move back and forth within the eternal stream linking past, present and future. The wolf-like beast controls the direction and the pace of change.

As long as there are no newcomers intruding on and disrupting its mystical order, the mountain will sustain everything that lives here, and the beast will continue to protect it.

But that is about to change.

SUMMER 2021

Annie and Will

In the valley, lights sparkled in the windows of houses clustered in busy neighborhoods. The sounds of pre-holiday activities carried in the night air. Children were shrieking, adults laughing and dogs barking at the explosion of backyard fireworks. On the nearby mountain, it was quiet. Clouds hung low over the pine trees that formed a border below the ridge.

Midway between the bustling and the silence, a white SUV, suitcases strapped to its top, moved slowly along a narrow, twisted road just below the timberline but well above the valley homes, headlight beams piercing the darkness. The Hartley family was arriving for the Fourth of July weekend that would be the beginning of their summer vacation. This year they had chosen to spend two weeks at a mountain cabin located near the edge of a forest, enjoying as much as they could of relatively unspoiled nature.

Annie sat in the back seat with her older brother, Will, peering at the shadowy landscape they were passing through. Without streetlights, every shape along the way seemed ominous. "This place looks really spooky, Dad. Are you sure we're on the right road?" Norman Hartley chuckled. His wife was alongside him in the front seat. "We're almost there, Annie. You're going to like it, I promise."

ANNIE felt fingers beginning to encircle her neck, tickling and momentarily startling her. "Will, cut it out!" She swirled to slap at her brother. He poked back. "You're such a baby," he laughed, as if the three-year difference in their ages mattered. The scuffle between them continued until their father started to inch their SUV cautiously up a steep driveway, bringing it to a stop in front of a small garage. She flung open her car door, leapt out, and ran up the short walkway leading to the log house perched at the top of the hill.

"Be careful!" her father shouted. "There may be some animals hidden in the dark."

"I can see perfectly well, Dad. There's plenty of moonlight." A rustling in the trees bordering the walkway made her stop. Were there eyes glinting from within the leaves? Some sort of forest creature? The rustling stopped and Annie continued up the walkway. Bounding up weathered wooden stairs, she scurried to the corner of the deck that wrapped around the cabin. "You won't believe the view from here!" she called to the others.

"You'll have plenty of time to explore tomorrow, Annie," her father called back. "Now, let's all just unpack and get some sleep. It's been a long day."

Annie looked one more time at the lights twinkling below in the valley. Then she turned around and gazed at the mountain looming dark behind her.

"I think I'm going to like this place," she said to herself, and ran back to join the others as they unpacked the car and prepared to settle into their new quarters.

What's Up There?

"Will, get out here fast. I already have my stuff."

The early morning air was damp and close, but that didn't keep Annie inside. She was always the first one out the door. Today, she and her brother had decided to spend some time on the deck. She was ten years old—ten going on eleven, as she liked to tell everyone. Curious and full of energy, she loved to do new things and explore new settings. Not like Will, who usually held back and sized up situations carefully before acting.

Their mother had told them to go outside for a while and enjoy the view while she tidied up the cabin, put luggage away, and got the place ready for their vacation. Will and Annie were glad to have the chance to take in their new surroundings, read a bit, and plan their adventures.

Annie peered back through the screen door of the cabin and called again. "William! What are you doing? We don't have all day!"

Actually, they did. School had been out for three weeks, and the summer stretched ahead. But Annie didn't want to waste time dawdling. Dawdling was Will's specialty, his way of telling her that he didn't take orders from his little sister. He knew it annoyed her.

No matter their differences, they both loved to read. On every vacation, they brought some of their favorite books and comics with them. Today on the rickety outdoor furniture on the deck, they would read until some other activity appealed to them.

"You didn't just bring all the girl stuff, did you?" Will shouted from inside the cabin. He didn't want to waste his time on the Disney stories they could see at their local movie theater. He was too old for that. Heck, he was going to turn thirteen in a couple of weeks. He'd much rather read stories about science. Anything about science. He had read *The Reinvention of Thomas Edison* earlier in the year and told his parents he wanted to be a physicist or an engineer when he grew up.

"I DIDN'T bring any of your books, dummy. Get them yourself!" Annie yelled back as she flung herself into a deck chair. What she wanted to be when she grew up was the last thing on Annie's mind. She just loved books. Especially mysteries. She and Will had talked about forming their own detective agency sometime. Anna and William Hartley Detectives, Inc.

"Whoa, it's hot out here," Will said, as he opened the screen door and came outside, balancing in one hand several of the favorites he had brought with him as he carefully closed the door with the other. It was a muggy day. More than usual, even for this time of year.

"What do you want to do if it doesn't rain?" Annie looked up at the dark clouds gathering overhead, black and billowy. The kind that brought storms, she had learned in school that year. Lightning crackled in the distance, the rumble of slow thunder following.

Will glanced up the mountain behind their cabin. "What about up there?" he said, assessing the thick wooded area that angled sharply upward.

"That's pretty steep," Annie said. She squinted her eyes and tried to focus on the detail of the terrain. "And very rocky." She looked harder into the distance. "Wait a minute. What's that up there?" she said, pointing to the top of the ridge. "It looks like some sort of house. Can you see it?"

Will's eyes followed where she was pointing. He stared at the shadowy structure. It had an unusual style, vaguely like something they had seen at Disney World during last summer's vacation.

"It could be a house," he said. "I can't tell from here. Looks kind of like a mansion, doesn't it? Why don't we check it out sometime?"

"Let's do it!"

THE ADVENTURE would have to wait a while. Rain descended on them in a sudden squall and forced them to take cover inside. By early afternoon the storm had passed by, but dark clouds still lingered atop the mountain. The ridge was enveloped in fog and a light mist now settled over the cabin and the deck.

"We could still go," Will said as they sat in the dining room of the cabin looking out the window. From there, they had a better sense of the difficulty of their hike up to the ridge.

They had been left pretty much to themselves. Their mother was taking a nap in one of the bedrooms, while their father had gone to the small town in the valley to get something for their evening meal. They were on their own for a while. Hartley Detectives Inc., free to explore. "I want to try it," Annie said.

They set out, startled at first by a couple of deer who darted across their path and headed up the slope. Will laughed. "We must have scared them."

Annie nodded. "They don't seem to like being around humans."

Once they felt certain the deer were no longer near them, they continued up the mountain, carefully picking their way through rocks, undergrowth and a thicket of oak brush that led to taller and more heavily clustered trees.

Will looked back to see if Annie was keeping up with him, and then turned his attention to what lay ahead of them. He glanced from side to side, trying to find a less slippery path. "Do you think we should keep going?"

"Of course! Why stop now?"

Soon they were well into the forest. The sun, which had broken through the mist in the first part of their hike, couldn't be seen in the thick stand of pines and spruce. Bright beams penetrated the woods in patches, but most of the area was covered in shadows and dense fog.

"Look over there, Annie!" Will, with his longer strides, was a few paces ahead of her. He peered into a grove to his left.

A trio of deer—a doe and two fawns—stood beneath the trees. Tannish brown with white-tipped tails, they had huge ears, pink inside, and looked quite different from the larger white-faced deer that roamed the foothills back home. The fawns gazed at Annie, their brown eyes unflinching. She loved animals—all animals—but she knew better than to approach them any closer. No telling what they might do if they were frightened.

"These don't look like the ones we saw earlier. Have they been following us all along?" she whispered.

"I don't know. I just noticed them. They may have been with us since we entered the woods."

"Look how big their ears are," she giggled.

The deer and the two children stood motionless for several minutes, staring at each other. Annie realized the fawns weren't frightened at all. It was like they had a connection with her. "The other deer ran away when they saw us," she whispered. "These don't. That's kind of strange."

Finally, the doe began a slow retreat, taking her young with her. One of the fawns—the smaller of the two—looked back, met Annie's gaze again and then turned, almost reluctantly, to follow the others farther into the woods.

Annie and Will proceeded up the slope, their progress still slowed by ferns and other undergrowth made slippery by the thick canopy of leaves dripping with moisture from the morning's rain. The woods finally gave way to a clearing, where they stood for a moment, breathing hard and straining to see in the fog. It had taken longer than they thought it would to reach the top of the ridge.

They looked around in surprise at what they saw—and what they didn't see. The house wasn't there.

"Did we mess up?" Will wondered. "Did we come up the wrong way?"

"No, look back there—down the mountain. You can still see the roof of our cabin—barely." Annie pointed at the path they had followed. "And that's the way we came up, through the trees. The house should be here. Or close enough that we could see it."

There was nothing but open space, framed by small, twisted trees and ground shrub, dark shapes that now seemed curious and strange. A moss-covered boulder lay to the side of the clearing.

"I don't like the way this feels, Annie," Will said. "Let's go back."

"O.K. But let's come back tomorrow. The weather might be better."

[21]

The trip back down the mountain was quicker, but more precarious. With the mist hanging over the mountain, the rocks were even wetter than they had been when Annie and Will had started up the slope. The two children arrived back at the cabin just in time to join their family for dinner.

Later, Will called Annie back out onto the cabin deck. Rain and fog had given way to a clear, brisk night, and a full moon illuminated the view. "Look. Up there. It's back," he said pointing at the ridge.

Annie glanced up and saw the house silhouetted against the sky just as it had been before they climbed the mountain.

"What the.... That's creepy," she said. "We really do need to go up there again," she said in her firmest voice. And then she turned to Will and said more softly, in amazement, "I bet that place has a really interesting story."

1910

Something Went Wrong

First there was a flash of light, bright and crackling, blue beams shooting out through the basement window of the stately two-story home. A sharp pop of electricity followed, heard several houses away.

Bertha Hemingway was like others in her small Ohio town, before radio broadcasts became widespread and before television was invented. She entertained herself by sitting in a rocking chair on the front porch of her bungalow, watching the activities of other people in the neighborhood. She was the first to report to the local police the strange spectacle across the street from her home.

"There are some frightening lights and noises coming out of the Hansinger house again," she said, shouting into the mouthpiece of the telephone mounted on the wall in her kitchen. "I think we all may be in some kind of danger." Neighbors listening on Bertha's party line chimed in, echoing her fears.

WITHIN a few minutes, sirens blaring, a police car and a fire truck arrived at the scene of the emergency Bertha had described. Elliott Hansinger stood at the front door of his home as a policeman and three firemen raced up the front steps. His clothes were rumpled and soiled, and he was waving his arms frantically. "Thank God you're here!" he exclaimed. "There's been an accident. My wife is missing."

Police Sergeant Bill Gerhardt was a veteran on the local force, ordinarily accustomed to handling misdemeanors like cattle blocking country roads outside town and the town drunk getting into bar fights on Saturday evenings. This case was clearly different. Bill knew immediately that it was going to be a difficult situation. He also sensed that he wouldn't get any useful information from Elliott without calming him down.

"Let's find a comfortable place where you can tell me what happened," he said in a soothing voice.

Elliott showed him into the living room off to the side of the front entry and the two men settled on couches facing each other. Bill began by quietly asking a few questions about the house. Harder questions could follow, after he had Elliott's confidence.

As the two men talked, a couple of the firemen who had followed Bill into the residence headed for the basement, while another did a quick search through the rooms on the main floor. Elaine Hansinger, Elliott's wife, couldn't be found, but the Hansinger's two children were discovered awake and trembling in one of the upstairs bedrooms. Eight-year-old Ben and his three-year-old sister Lizzy were brought to the living room where they sat at the side of the room and watched their father try to describe what had gone wrong that evening. Bill's questions became more pointed, zeroing in on Elliott's wandering story. He couldn't—or wouldn't—be specific about what had happened to Elaine.

"Are you suggesting I'm responsible for the disappearance of my wife?" Elliott got up from his couch and moved next to the fireplace. He waved his hands, pointing at Bill and the firemen who now stood waiting in the corner of the room. He wasn't used to being doubted. And he wasn't usually this agitated. He was a scholar, a professor at the local college. His life had been devoted to careful analysis and measured responses to problems.

"I'm not suggesting anything," Bill said. "But your answers are very vague. Evasive. You have to level with us."

"Leave me alone so I can try to find her," Elliott pleaded

and covered his face with his hands. "Or do something to help me," he said.

Ben looked over at Lizzy. Both were wide eyed. They'd never seen their father act like this. His lack of control frightened them. Ben wrapped his arm around Lizzy's shoulder and pulled her close.

With a deep sigh, Bill turned to the children. "Did you see any strange lights?" he asked. His tone was quiet and gentle.

"No. We were in our bedrooms, sleeping," Ben answered for his sister. She clung to him, shivering and crying softly, hugging the teddy bear that was her bedtime companion.

"Did any noises wake you up?" The policeman asked.

Ben nodded. "Yes."

"And where was your mother?"

"In our parent's bedroom, I guess. I don't know."

"Do you know where she is now?" the policeman persisted.

At this, Ben's voice wavered. "No."

Elliott walked over to his son and daughter and knelt, pulling both into his embrace. After a few moments, he rose and turned to face Bill.

"You're upsetting my children with your questions. My answers may seem vague because I really can't explain what happened. This is all I know: Elaine was with me," he said, struggling to control his voice. "In my laboratory downstairs. In the basement. She often assisted with my experiments. I trusted her."

"So, what happened? Why isn't she here now?"

[27]

Elliott ran his hand through his hair and stared down at the floor. When he looked up again, his face was twisted into a frown. "We were working on some ideas I had about energy fields. And we were taking turns adjusting the equipment." He paused. "Something went wrong. She just rotated one of the dials and suddenly there was a bright flash, a pop of electricity and...she disappeared."

"Disappeared?"

"One moment she was there and then there was the blaze of light, and she was gone."

Lizzy huddled in her chair, sobbing and shaking, still holding her teddy bear tight. Elliott knelt next to her again and pulled her to him, patting her on the back and stroking her hair.

"Don't worry, Lizzy. We'll bring her back. I promise."

Moving On

The active police probe of Elaine Hansinger's disappearance wrapped up rather quickly. The case wasn't closed, but Bill Gerhardt didn't have any evidence that a crime had actually been committed. In the basement of the Hansinger residence, which Elliott claimed was his laboratory, the police found nothing but a few small boxes with dials, some odd pieces of electrical equipment and a large closet-like enclosure on a side wall. Scorch marks next to one of the electrical boxes were the only remnants of the bright flash and noises that had disturbed Bertha Hemingway and her neighbors. Nothing there suggested that anyone other than Elliott had been in the basement when the incident occurred.

There was no question that Elaine was missing, but Elliott's description of the way she disappeared was just too unbelievable. Bizarre.

"You know what I think happened, Kevin?" Bill was leaning back in his desk chair at the police station, enjoying a cup of coffee and reviewing the details of the case with Kevin Rutgers, his partner on the investigation. "I think Elaine just got tired of her husband's strangeness and left him."

Kevin pondered Bill's comment and nodded slowly. "He is an odd duck, isn't he?"

MANY IN the community shared that impression of Elliott Hansinger, including his colleagues at the college. His "research," as he liked to call it, had nothing to do with his faculty position in engineering. It was more like a hobby. He spent hours in the basement of his home tinkering with electrical contraptions and radio waves. He bored almost everyone he knew with his speculations about a future that he was convinced would be transformed by inventions involving greater use of electricity.

"I wouldn't blame her if she did," Kevin replied. "But she wouldn't leave her kids behind, would she?"

"No. Everyone says she was a good mother. But maybe they had a fight or something and she just left for a while, meaning to come back. Maybe all the fuss at the house, with the neighbors calling us and all, just made their personal problems too public. From everything I've heard, from Bertha Hemingway and others who knew her, she was a very private and shy woman. She may have been too embarrassed to face people after her troubles with Elliott became known."

"Well, that's just a guess, Bill. We really don't know where she is now. But it is interesting that her parents are insisting on moving the kids to the place where Elaine grew up."

"Leaving Elliott here by himself," Bill added. The story was the object of gossip throughout the neighborhood.

"How did the two of them meet anyway? Elliott and Elaine? This is a long way from that town out west."

"According to Bertha Hemingway, Elaine came to study at the college. Met Elliott when he was a student too, I guess. She was one of the few women taking science classes there. Biology mainly. Actually, one of few women at the college. They must have found they had some interests in common."

"What else do we know about him anyway? Like—how can he afford that house? It's nicer by far than everything else in that section of town. And what about all that electrical stuff? The house has all the latest gadgets. They're not cheap."

"Bertha says Elaine told her that Elliott lost his mother when he was very young. And then he inherited a lot of money when his father died several years ago. He was an only child. So, he's pretty well off."

The two men were silent for a while. Bill sipped his coffee and Kevin stared out the window. "It bothers me that we don't have any clue about where she is. Elliott was truly upset that she had disappeared, so I don't think he harmed her. That's just my gut feeling. But his story about how she disappeared is so far-fetched. Maybe he blacked out for a long time or something. She got scared."

"We'll keep an eye on him," Kevin assured him.

*E*LAINE'S PARENTS, Bert and Louise Smith, came by train from their home in a mountain valley in Utah and took Ben and Lizzy back to live with them. Elliott stayed in Ohio until the school year ended. Bertha and her friends managed to keep track of what he was doing through gossip that circulated rather freely among them. They learned that he had quit his job at the college. Shortly after that, he closed up his house and prepared to move.

Watching from her front porch, Bertha saw men come to put in crates many books, a few pieces of furniture and the family's clothing, carrying the crates away in a truck, probably to a warehouse where they would be stored until they could be shipped. Elliott left soon after that. That was the last that Bertha and her friends thought about Elliott and his family. They soon had other things to talk about.

Bill Gerhardt and Kevin Rutgers had other matters to investigate, but from time to time they turned their attention once again to the mysterious disappearance of Elaine Hansinger.

"That's the strangest case I have ever encountered on this job," Bill said to Kevin one day when they were speculating about what had happened. "I wonder if we will ever find out what became of her?"

"I'm not going to let it drop," Kevin vowed. "I'm going to keep looking, no matter how long it takes."

A New Home

Elliott stayed in touch with Ben and Lizzy by mail, writing to them every day—usually short notes saying how much he loved and missed them. But he sent the news of his trip by telegram to Elaine's parents:

TRAIN ARRIVES SATURDAY 1 PM (stop) EAGER

TO SEE BEN AND LIZZY (stop) LOVE, E

Bert read the message aloud to Louise and shrugged. "We can't very well keep him away from the children. He's their father, after all."

They didn't like Elliott. Never did, even when Elaine brought him home to meet them before the wedding. "He's pretty much out of touch with reality," Bert had told Elaine. "I don't doubt he loves you, but I don't think he is capable of providing you with a normal, stable marriage."

Elaine didn't agree. She was in awe of Elliott's intelligence. What others regarded as strange, she found interesting. So she went ahead with the wedding. "I love him, and he loves me," she told her parents. "I know he's a bit unusual, but he would do anything for me."

Her parents kept their concerns to themselves after that. Now, however, Elaine's strange disappearance reawakened their fears about him. They wanted Ben and Lizzy to continue to live with them, where it would be safe. Safe from whatever had taken Elaine away from her children and her family. Even though they had no reason to doubt the results of the police investigation, they still felt Elliott was responsible in some way for whatever had happened to Elaine. The only reason they didn't discourage him from coming out west was the obvious love and bond he shared with Ben and Lizzy.

The day his train was scheduled to arrive, Bert and Louise took the two children to the station.

"Daddy!" Lizzy squealed when she saw him. "Daddy! I missed you!" She ran toward him, with Ben following close behind her. Elliott put his suitcases down on the platform and knelt, arms spread wide. Lizzy fell into his embrace. Ben joined in the hug.

𝓐 SLEEPING AREA had been prepared in the basement of the Smith's house to serve as his bedroom, but Elliott knew he wasn't welcome. His first night there, after Ben and Lizzy had gone to bed, the three adults confronted each other in the elegant living room.

Elaine had told Elliott repeatedly how much she loved the Victorian furnishings in her parents' home, a legacy of the family's privileged past inherited from Louise's mother. Lamps with hand-dyed embroidered shades, beaded trims and hand-strung glass beads cast a soft light over the upholstered sofa and matching accent chairs that formed a conversation area. Doilies Louise had tatted adorned the marble-topped coffee table and the accent cabinets in the corners and along one of the side walls.

Elaine's parents and Elliott settled uncomfortably into seats opposite each other. Bert and Louise broke the awkward silence insisting that Elliott tell them what had happened to their daughter. His answer was the same explanation he had given to the police.

"Your story is crazy. You don't seriously expect us to believe it!" Bert said.

"It's the truth!" Elliott replied, struggling to keep his voice under control. "I don't know how to convince you."

"So, if she disappeared the way you say she did, in a flash of electricity, where is she now?" Louise demanded.

"I don't know. But I have a theory...."

"A theory? What do you mean?"

"I think she's in another dimension. Another reality...."

"Oh, for heaven's sake. I refuse to listen to this nonsense!" Louise rose and walked out of the room, leaving Bert and Elliott staring at each other.

"Bert, I know this is hard for you to accept. It is for me too, but you must believe me. I'd give anything—do anything—if I could bring Elaine back. And I'm going to keep trying to find a way to do that."

*E*LLIOTT SPENT as much time as he could with Ben and Lizzy the next couple of months. The mild summer weather was ideal for their explorations of the mountain that overlooked the town. It had been a place where Elaine had hiked and gone on picnics with school friends when she was young. He remembered how she told him that her treks up the mountain had kindled her curiosity about animals and the vegetation that sustained them. "That's how I got interested in biology," she had said. "I felt at home with the varieties of life I found there."

Several times, Elliott took Ben and Lizzy up to the wooded area that dominated the slope. There were days when he knew his children wanted to be with their friends in their new home, so he spent the time by himself, away from Bert and Louise and the tension that filled every interaction he had with them.

He went on long hikes up the mountain. He loved the musky smell of nestling animals and the earthy aroma of the sheltering trees. The sensations he had when he was deep in the forest stirred his imagination. He felt a mystical calm there, a sense that he was in another world of some kind. He even began to fantasize that some of the animals who had earlier stayed away from him now welcomed him into their midst.

One day late in July, sitting on a boulder in a clearing that had become his favorite spot to rest, he saw a doe watching him from the protective cover of the trees. And then he froze. Heart pounding, he watched as a scraggly creature moved stealthily past the doe and stopped a few feet away from him, growling, teeth bared. It stared at him and pawed at the ground before scampering away, leaving behind a strong, musty wet fur smell that Elliott would come to recognize whenever the creature came near again.

Later in the summer, as Elliott sat cross legged on the boulder, eyes closed, meditating, it happened, the thing he had most wanted in the tortured months since Elaine had disappeared. He heard her voice calling to him.

He looked around. He couldn't see her, but he knew she was there. Bewildered, he shook his head and tried to understand what was happening.

Her voice came to him again, louder and clearer. "Elliott. Come find me."

From that day forward, he knew what he would have to do. Somehow, he would build a house on the mountain, maybe even at the top. A home for himself and for Ben and Lizzy. A place where Elaine could return to him.

THE PORTAL

Was It a Dream?

In the evening, sprawled in front of the TV in the front room of the cabin, the Hartley family gathered to view a Harry Potter DVD they had brought with them.

Will lay on the floor, his head and neck propped against the convertible sofa that would later be his bed. Annie was sprawled on a brown stuffed bean bag that nearly swallowed her up as she snuggled in it to watch the movie. Halfway through *The Chamber of Secrets,* Will fell asleep, snoring. It didn't matter, really. They'd all seen the movie several times before. Annie and her parents stuck with it until the familiar ending.

After that, they opened the sofa bed and Will rolled onto it, as his mother brought out an extra pillow from their bedroom. Annie, still wired from the day's excitement, headed to the small room at the back of the cabin that was her bedroom. She didn't like to sleep in a closed space, so she left her window slightly open, letting in the cold mountain air and the sound of trees rustling. Sitting for a time on the edge of her bed, her elbows propped on the windowsill, she gazed at the moonlit landscape outside. It was so calm and peaceful, really. Why had it seemed so frightening at the top of the mountain?

She climbed into bed and pulled the covers up to her chin. There, she lay awake for a long time. She couldn't stop thinking about the mysterious house and the trip she and Will had made up the mountain. And what should she make of the deer who had accompanied them along the way? Their brown eyes, watching and knowing...knowing what?

As she began to drift to sleep, images from the afternoon filled her dream. She was back up at the top of the mountain, standing in the clearing in front of the house. Three deer watched from a copse of trees. And then she was back in the cabin again.

Halfway between sleep and wakefulness, she heard a tapping sound coming from outside the open window. She pulled a pillow over her head to muffle the noise, but the tapping continued, even louder. She couldn't escape it, so she got up and looked out the window to the ground below.

There, gazing quietly back at her were the two big-eared fawns she had seen on the mountain.

"Come help us," a voice said, not aloud but in Annie's head.

"How?" Annie replied, and the minute she said it, she was outside with the deer.

"Who are you?" she asked.

They said nothing. They just stared back at her with puzzled looks.

"Can you understand me?" she asked.

One of the fawns looked like it was about to speak but stopped. Then the deer were gone. And Annie was back in her bed. She buried her head in her pillow, and she could feel her heart pounding. What was happening to her? If this was a dream, she had never had one that was so strange and vivid.

She sat up and looked around, trying to see something familiar in the darkness. It was pitch black in her room, although the moon still shone on the landscape outside. Scratching and skittering sounds came from beneath the cabin, probably from small animals foraging in the night. It was too much for her. She pulled her pillow over her ears and closed her eyes tight. Exhausted, she fell asleep.

The next morning, she shuffled out to the kitchen, groggy and half awake. Will, sitting at the breakfast table, was already dressed for the day, although as usual his hair was uncombed and messy. Hunched over his bowl of Cheerios, he looked up when Annie plopped down in a chair opposite him at the table with her own bowl of Frosted Flakes and a glass of orange juice.

They didn't talk much. Will was always quiet in the morning, so Annie gazed out the window at the town she could see down in the valley, frowning as she tried to make sense of what had happened to her overnight.

Finally, scooping up a spoonful of cereal, Will glanced at Annie, careful to assess her mood before he spoke.

"How did you sleep?"

"Not very well. I had a strange dream."

"About what?"

"We were at the top of the mountain. And the house was there."

Will looked at her, the spoon he was holding suspended midway between the cereal bowl and his mouth.

"The deer were there too," Will prompted. "And then a couple of them were here—at the cabin."

Annie looked back at him. "You won't believe what else happened."

"Don't tell me," he said. "I know. You heard one of them speak."

They stared open-mouthed at each other. They had had the same dream.

Will lifted the bowl to his mouth and slurped its contents before he put it back on the table. He wiped milk from his chin and held his finger to his mouth, signaling to his sister. "Shhh."

It was only a dream about animals they had seen on the mountain, but it was too disturbing and real. Why had it come to both of them on the same night? This was scary in a way that they couldn't explain, not to anyone, and especially not to their parents. What to do next was clear, however. There would be no sitting on the deck this morning.

They glanced over at their father, sitting in the area next to the kitchen that was set aside for lounging.

"Dad, we're going back up the mountain again, to see what's at the top," Will said. "Is that o.k.?"

Wearing a rumpled sweatshirt and jeans, his hair spiked and unkempt, just like Will's, their father sprawled on the sofa, engrossed in a book on the history of the nearby town. He turned a page and looked up just long enough to mumble.

"Mmmph. Just don't be gone too long."

W HETHER OF not he had heard them wasn't clear. But at least he hadn't told them they couldn't do what they were planning to do.

Their mom was likely to be a harder sell. She actually listened to them most of the time. She was cleaning up after breakfast.

"Mom—we're going to take another hike in the woods—up the mountain behind us."

Evelyn Hartley looked at them and smiled. She was an older image of her children—a blend of the two. She was tall and slender like Will, but she had Annie's sandy hair and blue eyes. And, like Annie, she loved to explore. She knew how it felt, always to be on the lookout for adventure. But she also knew how impulsive her daughter could be.

"I want you to promise me that, if you run into anything that doesn't look safe, you will turn around and come back here immediately."

"We will Mom. We promise."

"Well then, have fun. But be back for lunch. Don't stay up there as long as you did yesterday."

Mission approved, Will and Annie darted out the front door, stopping just long enough to grab the backpacks they had brought with them, filled with first-aid kits, water, and granola bars. Once outside the cabin, they followed the trail they knew would take them to the top of the ridge. This morning, the path was familiar and dry, and the sun was shining brightly. With better climbing conditions, they easily reached the clearing they had found the day before. There, where it had not been the day before, was the strange house they had seen from the deck of their cabin.

It wasn't at all impressive up close. The paint on its siding was gray and cracked in places. On several of the windows at the front of the house, the shutters hung loose, flapping in the light wind that was blowing across the ridge. It was two stories tall. An expansive porch ran across the entire length of the house, framed by fluted columns.

There may have been a time when it was a showcase of sorts, but no more. Now, all that was left of that elegance were hints of what used to be. The place looked almost forlorn. Clearly no one lived there now, and probably hadn't for some time.

"I want to go inside," Annie said to Will. "There doesn't seem to be anyone around who would mind."

"Uh...Annie, this is somebody's house. We shouldn't just barge in like we own the place." Will chewed on his lower lip and looked around. "Let's just peek in the windows."

"Will, you are so lame! There's nobody here. And we aren't going to be here long."

"This is somebody's house. Private property!"

*A*NNIE WAS already running toward the front steps, bounding up them two at a time. Will held back for a few seconds, looking from left to right, chewing on his lip even more. Looking down at the ground at first, he scuffed his shoes in the loose rocks that were scattered on the approach to the house. Then he sighed and hurried after his sister.

The front door was solid oak, with two small leaded glass windows. Annie grabbed the large brass doorknob. It didn't turn easily at all, but she kept twisting it. When she leaned her shoulder into the door and pushed against it, she could feel it begin to budge.

"Come on and help me, Will. I think we might be able to get it open."

Will hesitated, watching as Annie kept pushing against the door with her shoulder.

"Ooof! I can feel it start to move."

The aged wood of the door frame gave way with a snap and the door swung open, revealing a small entryway. In the background, a curving staircase led to a second floor.

"Omigosh. Look what we've done!" Will stepped back, refusing to go inside the house that was now open but not actually inviting them, at least not in his eyes.

Annie stepped across the threshold and peered around. The musty smell of dust and mold that greeted her in the entryway confirmed her suspicion that it had been closed for a very long time.

Looking back at the trees they had passed through on their way up the mountain, Will thought for a minute about heading back to the cabin. "If you run into anything that makes you feel unsafe, turn around and come back immediately," their mother had told them. Well, that's exactly what he was feeling right now. But he couldn't—wouldn't—leave Annie here by herself. So he slowly followed his sister into the house. And sneezed. Then he sneezed again.

"You know I'm allergic to dust," he said in a loud whisper. "I can't stay here very long."

"Well then, stay close to the door. There's fresh air coming in there."

With Will pinned in the entry hall, Annie tiptoed into the room that lay to her left.

"Omigosh. This is incredible."

It was a grand library, taking up the length of the front on the left side of the house, and extending almost all the way to the back. Squinting in the dim light that filtered through the partially shuttered windows, Annie could see floor-to-ceiling bookcases filled with volumes in all shapes and sizes. The furniture, arranged mainly in the center of the room, was draped with white sheets—ghostly protection against dust and any insects that found their way into the house through the fireplace that took up almost half of the wall at the end of the room. The bookcases were pine, and the floors were oak. The entire room was a picture of permanence, stability and strength.

"Look at this. The fireplace is huge. Big enough that I can stand inside it."

Huge didn't even begin to describe the fireplace. Monumental. Massive. Made entirely of granite rocks that had probably been taken from the mountain outside, it had a cavernous opening blackened with soot. A large set of andirons stood to the side, but there was no screen in front of the grate that now held the ashes of long-dead fires. A large stone lion's head embellished the top of the curved opening of the fireplace. On a side wall hung a mounted, stuffed head of a male deer with enormous antlers.

Annie was looking up the chimney when Will finally decided to follow her into the library.

"There's no opening," she said, standing in the fireplace and looking up.

"What do you mean?"

"I mean there is no opening in the chimney. It's been covered up. Or stopped up with something."

"That isn't possible. There couldn't be any fires in there. The smoke would back up and fill up the room."

"So come here and take a look! Honestly, you never believe me."

Will stepped into the mouth of the fireplace and gazed upward. Annie was right. The opening to the chimney was clogged with twigs and some sort of overgrown plant that had taken up root inside it.

A sharp popping sound startled them, followed by an acrid smell and a tingling, prickly sensation that overcame both. The hair on their heads begin to stand on end.

"Can you feel that? It's like electricity—some sort of energy," Will said in a shaky voice.

Annie said nothing. Her eyes and her mouth were open wide. She grabbed her brother's hand.

The house began to vibrate. As it did, the sheets covering the furniture fluttered and danced and the bookcases began to sway.

"Wh...h...a...t's happening?" Annie whispered.

"I don't know but we're getting out of here. NOW!"

They stumbled back across the room, through the entry hall and out the front door onto the porch. The shuddering and shaking grew worse, accompanied by a loud rumble. Gathering their strength, they leaped off the front porch and rolled onto the ground just beyond the front steps—or where the front steps had just been. They scrambled toward each other and looked back.

"Omigosh, omigosh. Can you see...?"

"Yeah, but I don't believe it."

The house was gone.

Is This Real?

They sat on the ground for a few moments. Will checked his elbows and hands. They felt a little sore, but at least they weren't scraped or bloody from the fall. He looked over at his sister. Annie rubbed her knees, which were painful but not bleeding. "Let's go back to the cabin," she said. "I don't like what is going on here!"

Will rose, pulled Annie to her feet and helped her dust off her jeans, now torn and covered with dirt. They picked up the backpacks that had fallen a few feet away from them.

As they looked around for the path to their cabin, they saw that they were not alone. The three deer they had encountered the day before were standing at the edge of the clearing. Their eyes were once again locked on the two children, but as soon as they were noticed, the deer turned and started to walk slowly into the woods. Then they stopped and looked back. One of the fawns stared at Annie.

"I think they want us to go along with them," she said.

"Do you think it's safe?" Will asked.

"I don't know. I wonder where they are leading us?" There was something in the fawn's gaze that was reassuring. "I think they may be trying to help."

The doe's eyes shifted to Annie. There was a flicker of something in her gaze that almost seemed like agreement.

"You may be right. Let's follow them. If it doesn't feel right, we can stop."

And so, the unlikely group wound down the mountain, carefully now, as mist had moved in to make the trail even more slippery. It was hard to follow, spreading over rocks and thick undergrowth. Annie stumbled and almost fell. She grabbed Will's arm to keep her balance. "Let's stop!"

she cried out. "It feels strange here. Something is different."

Will hesitated, looking around at the trees that surrounded them. The deer didn't seem to notice, instead moving slowly ahead until they finally disappeared into the fog that now shrouded everything.

"If we're not sure where we're going, we need to figure out what to do," Will said, looking around for a place to sit. He settled on a large boulder over to the side of the path and set his backpack down beside it. Annie stood briefly, and then found another boulder close to him where she could perch. Stiff and bruised from their leap off the porch, they both welcomed the chance to rest. It also gave them time to pull their thoughts together. They stared in silence at the murky blanket that enveloped them.

FINALLY, Annie spoke. "I'm sorry I didn't listen to you. We were lucky we didn't get hurt."

"Yeah, well, you do some crazy things sometimes. Don't you ever think about what might happen?"

Annie lowered her head and gazed for a moment at the ground. Then she looked back up, her jaw set firm. "Don't tell me you weren't curious about what was in the house! And why we kept seeing it and not seeing it. Didn't you want to find out what really happened up there?" She glared at Will.

They were quiet for a long time before her brother spoke again. "Should we tell Mom and Dad?" Will asked.

"We'll probably get in trouble if we do. I know I'll get in trouble if we do."

Will wasn't about to disagree. He always seemed to be pulling Annie out of danger or covering for some fix she had gotten them both into. But she was right. He had been curious too. He wanted to know more. And Annie as usual was the one who made sure they found out.

An idea came to him. "Maybe we could get Dad to take us to the library in town. And maybe somebody there will be able to tell us something about the house. We're probably not the only ones who have seen it. There must be some story about it that people know."

"Yes! We could investigate! I like that! But first we have to get back to the cabin."

They looked around as they tried to figure out how to reach the trail they had followed up the mountain. Finding it wouldn't be easy. The fog had closed in around them, and they faced a gray wall in every direction they looked, with only the hint of trees looming in the background.

Will rummaged in his backpack and found the compass he carried with him on Boy Scout camping trips. It wasn't very expensive, and he had never had to use it before. But it was all that he had right now, He looked down at it, and then glanced up, pointing his finger.

"That's south. That's where our cabin is. Let's go."

In the misty quiet of the landscape, they found their way back to a smoother path and started down the mountain once again. Everything was calm and still.

"It's kind of like walking through one of those dioramas at the Natural History Museum back home, isn't it?" Annie said. "I mean, it's all sort of lifelike, but not really."

"But the dioramas smell kind of musty," Will said, sniffing. "Here, I can smell the trees. And some animals. Can you?"

Annie spread her arms wide. "Yes! Everything is so fresh! I love it. I wish it could stay this way forever!"

Hidden in a stand of pine trees behind them, where they couldn't see him, the wolf-beast stood, listening. At Annie's words, he nodded his approval, and then turned and trotted quietly back up the mountain.

Ben and Lizzy

In the lower part of the forest, the fog was still thick. It was hard to see more than a few feet ahead, so Will took the lead, looking carefully from side to side for anything unusual. When they reached a clearing, he stopped.

"Did you hear that?" he said to Annie, but peering to his left, through the pine trees that lined the path they were taking.

Annie slowed and listened too. "It sounds like leaves rustling. Or wind blowing."

"No, it's not wind. But the leaves are being moved by something."

The sound quit for a minute—and was there again. A slight crackling of something in the undergrowth, and a whisper of movement. Suddenly, two figures emerged out of the mist—a boy and a girl, dressed in baggy pants, old-fashioned hats and cloth coats, looking like kids in old photos Annie had seen in a family album at her grandmother's house. The boy was tall and thin, dark haired, with deep brown eyes. He looked close to the same age as Will. Behind him, timid and quiet, was the little girl, probably a few years younger and very small, with straight blonde hair. The boy reached for her hand and pulled her close alongside him. And then he gave his full attention to Will and Annie.

"Who are you?" Annie said, blunt as usual.

"Who are you?" the boy answered. "I've never seen you around here before."

Will pulled his shoulders back to make his voice sound forceful. "Is that a problem?" he asked.

"Maybe not," the boy said, as he and the little girl resumed their slow walk forward. "We just never see people

[54]

we don't know around here. Strangers." He looked hard at Will. "You didn't answer my question. Who are you?" he repeated. He was struggling to be in control of the situation.

"We live in the cabin just down the mountain," Will said.

"What cabin?" the other boy said. "There's nothing around here but our house, up on the ridge."

"That's not true," Will said. "I'll show you." He walked over to the edge of the clearing and pointed in the direction of the cabin. Its roof had been just barely visible in the distance earlier in the day. He gasped and stepped back, grabbing Annie's arm.

It wasn't there anymore.

Will couldn't speak for a moment. Annie could tell that her brother was trying not to act scared.

ƁUT NOT Annie. She was just upset and frustrated.

"Look," she said to the other two children. "Something strange is going on. We really are staying in a cabin down there. I don't know why we can't see it now. But every-thing has been really weird all day. Ever since we hiked up the mountain this morning and saw the house on the ridge up there. And it disappeared after we were inside it."

The other boy stared at her.

"Did you say you were in our house? And it disap-peared after you were in it?"

"Yes. It started to shake and make loud noises. We got out of it as fast as we could," Will said. He was eager to join in the conversation. "When we looked back, it was gone."

The boy and girl looked at each other, and then at Will and Annie.

"I don't understand all that," the boy said. "But some strange things have happened to us today too," the boy continued. "When I got up for breakfast today, I couldn't find my father. He's usually busy in the house in the morning. Then I woke my sister up so she could help me look for him. He was gone."

No one spoke for a few moments, as they all tried to make sense of the stories they had shared. Finally, the boy held out his hand to Will. "My name is Ben. And this is Lizzy."

The two boys shook hands. "I'm Will. She's Annie."

"Where do you live? I mean, where do you come from?" Annie asked.

"We live here," Ben said. "We moved to this place from our home out east. Our father built our house at the top of the ridge. It was done this year."

"Why didn't you stay where you were before?" Annie asked. Will winced at his sister's way of forcing a conversation to get to the point. A softer tone was needed, he thought. Something to build trust.

"Look, let's everybody sit down," Will said, pointing to the fallen trees at the side of the open space where they stood. "We'll all be more comfortable, and it will be easier to talk."

They found their way to a spot where they could sit and face each other. Annie and Will settled on the ground. Lizzy perched on a log, crouching next to Ben.

Ben scuffed his shoe at the ground for a while and then he cleared his throat. He looked at Annie. "You wanted to know why we didn't stay where we came from. It's kind of hard to explain. We had a great life back there. Out east, I mean. We had a nice house there and everything. Father taught at the college. He's an engineer. But suddenly one day our mother went missing. In some sort of accident." Lizzy started to cry, and Ben patted her shoulder. "After that, Father decided he didn't want to stay there. So, he just quit his job and came here."

"Why did he choose this place?" Annie asked.

"The town in the valley is where our mother came from. We came to stay with our grandparents, and he followed us. We all lived with them until he finished the house on the ridge. He built it there because the mountain was special to our mother. He says it makes him feel close to her."

Ben stopped and focused his attention on Annie. "Lizzy and I didn't want to live up here at first. Our friends were all in the valley. And that's where we go to school. But Father makes the rules. We do what he says."

W ILL AND Annie glanced at each other. Ben's description of his relationship with his father was so unlike their own, it was hard to believe his story, but they decided not to question him about it. The silence grew awkward until Ben spoke again.

"O.K., now it's my turn to ask a question: where do you come from, and what did you mean when you said things today have been...what did you say? Weird? What else was weird besides what happened when you were in our house on the ridge?"

"It's a long story," Will answered. He described what had happened since he and Annie first came up the mountain. Annie kept interrupting him to add details. When it came to the part where the house disappeared and they got lost in the fog, Ben didn't speak, but his eyes were filled with alarm. He looked over at his sister. She was staring at the ground, trying not to cry.

"What did you do after you found your father missing?" Will asked, attempting to draw them out of their silence.

"Well, that's kind of hard to explain." Ben scratched his head and stared for a moment back up at the ridge. "First, we searched all through the house. Then we went outside, thinking he might be there. He wasn't, which was really scary. That's not like him to just leave without telling us where he was going. So, we decided to go back to the house. But we knew we wouldn't be able to stay there too long by ourselves. We had to find someone else to help us."

Ben looked at Will and Annie, hoping they understood the desperation he and his sister felt. "We've tried heading down into the valley," he continued, "to get help. From our grandparents, or anyone else we could find. But we kept getting lost. The fog was so thick and the rocks really big and we were going farther into the forest, not away from it. Everything looked so different. I mean, the forest wasn't the same." Ben's voice trembled. "I don't know how, but we ended up here in this spot in the woods."

Lizzy sniffled and wiped the tears from her eyes. Ben wrapped his arms around her and held her tight. Nobody spoke for several moments. Annie peered at the ground, thinking. She looked at Ben and Lizzy in their odd clothes, tried to make sense of their story about where they had come from, and felt pity for them for the loss of their mother. She stared at their strange clothing. Why was it so different? Why did they seem to be so unlike other kids her age?

She was about to ask about their clothes when Will said, "Can you help us find our way home?"

"We can at least show you another way down the mountain," Ben answered. "Maybe that will lead you to a place that looks familiar. Assuming the cabin is there...."

"What about us?" Lizzy asked. "What about finding Daddy?"

"We might be able to help each other, Lizzy," Annie said to reassure her and to reassure herself. She didn't feel that confident then, either. But it was comforting that she and Will had found two other children at a moment when they were also confused and concerned. The four of them might be able to solve their problems together.

"So that settles it," Ben said, and mustered a timid smile. "We'll follow the trail together. It will be an adventure."

"Before we do that, I think we may have another problem to worry about," Annie said. She was getting impatient. The day was slipping away. She wanted action.

"It's going to get dark in a few hours," she reminded them. "If we can't see how to get back to our cabin, we'll have no place to stay, and we don't have enough food. Will and I have a little in our backpacks, but it won't last us long."

"There's food in our kitchen," Lizzy said softly. "If we can find the house...." Her voice trailed off.

"Maybe that's what we should do next," Will said. He was in his element again in his self-appointed role as project organizer. "We have to go back to your place at the top of the ridge. I think that might be where the answer is."

"But what if the house isn't there? If you saw it disappear, maybe we won't be able to find it again." Ben said.

Annie thought for a moment. "Why do we assume the house is the key?" she asked.

"Where else could it be?" Ben asked. "The house is the only place we have in common."

"Is it?" Annie responded. Her brow was furrowed, her lips pinched. She needed to be convinced. "We both came to this clearing. Why is this where we ended up?"

"It's on a deer trail," Ben said. "Their tracks make a path that make it easy to get through the forest. And they're here a lot."

"HOW MANY are there?" Annie asked. The image of the deer that she and Will had seen on the mountain and in their dream came back to her.

"I don't know for sure. We've seen a bunch of them near the house. We used to think it was because Father had killed a buck last year. Its head is on a wall in our house."

"We saw deer on our way up the mountain and at our cabin," Will said. "And we were following them just before we ran into you and Lizzy."

There was silence as the four thought about what may have been just a coincidence. But if it wasn't…. Ben scratched his head again before he spoke. "I think I know where they were going. There's a canyon on the edge of these woods. Father showed it to me. He said he found it when he was out hunting. It leads to the valley."

"Well, I'd say it's worth a try," Will answered, changing their plan again. "Let's hike that way. If we end up somewhere in the valley, we might at least find somebody to help us."

With Ben in the lead, the four headed away from the clearing, across the mountain. What started as a fairly easy walk for them grew increasingly difficult as the undergrowth grew thicker and rocks broke up the trail they were trying to follow. Lizzy struggled to keep up with her brother. It was taking a long time to make their way through the forest.

"Look!" Ben suddenly shouted, pointing at the light flickering through the trees ahead of them. "There's another clearing."

"And that's sunlight," Annie said, her breath coming in short gasps. She was having trouble breathing in the thin mountain air. "We're leaving the fog."

Above them, the mid-afternoon sun shone, and the sky was bright blue and cloudless. They kept walking, Ben holding tight to Lizzy's hand, and Annie and Will clambering over the rocks alongside each other. Sunbeams angling through the gaps in the pine grove exposed a dirt road that lay ahead as the trees became smaller and less thick. The children ran toward it and followed it until they found themselves back on top of the ridge, approaching Ben and Lizzy's house from a different direction. They had somehow wound their way to the other side of the mountain.

The four of them rushed around to the front porch and bounded up the steps. Ben pushed open the heavy oak door and waved them in. Staggering into the entry way, they were overcome with exhaustion.

"Let's rest for a while in the library," Ben said, pointing to the door that opened off the entry way. Entering the room, he and Lizzy lay down on the couches in the center of a large book-filled room. Will and Annie headed for cushions on the floor in front of the huge stone fireplace.

Within minutes they were all sound asleep.

Where Are We?

Hands tucked under heads, legs curled up to chests, they awoke to late afternoon sunbeams slanting through the windows. Annie sat up, her thoughts jumbled by all that had happened. She grasped her forehead with both hands. Will rubbed his eyes and rose gradually to a kneeling position so he could get a better look at the huge room. A few feet away from them, Ben and Lizzy got up from their couches and stood, swaying slightly as they looked around.

"This place isn't old anymore," Will said, staring at the furniture and the wall hangings that dominated the middle section of the library. Annie scooted on her knees to a place next to her brother and stared at the scene. He was right. There were no sheets covering the furniture, no dusty books on the shelves. Everything was fresh-smelling, bright and new, with shiny surfaces. The lion's head stared out at the room from his place above the fireplace. The buck on the side wall had a gentler look, its brown eyes cast downward.

"I don't see anything different," Lizzy said. Ben nodded. "This is our home. It doesn't look like anything has changed."

Annie kept looking at the buck. He seemed kindly, but his antlers were huge. "He's such a beautiful animal," Annie said, moved by his gentle gaze. "He doesn't look like the deer that have been following us. I wish he could be alive and free again too." But she and Will had their own problems. She turned to Ben. "Did you say there was food in this house?"

"Is that all you can think about?" he snapped. "We've got other things to figure out. Like what's happened to all of us today."

"We're going to need food no matter what," Annie said, clenching her jaw and glaring back at him. "We don't know how long we're going to be here, or what we're going to have to do to get things back to normal. But we won't always have access to food, whatever we decide to do. So if there's any in this house, where is it?"

"She's right," Will said. "We do need to plan what we're going to do next. Whatever that is, we'll need a good food supply."

Ben sighed and headed toward a door at the end of the room, ending the argument. "There's food in the kitchen. Follow me."

Ben and Lizzy led the way down a hallway from the library. The kitchen was at the back of the house. They entered it through a swinging wooden door. Large built-in wooden cupboards were on every wall, and a counter extended on both sides of the sink at the opposite end of the room. A window above the sink opened the entire area to light from outside. The only other features were a black wood stove for cooking, alongside a shiny appliance that looked like an old refrigerator.

"That's an icebox," Will whispered to Annie, pointing. "I've read about them!"

He looked around, his brow furrowed. "I wish I had that cell phone Dad said he is going to get me for my birthday. I could call Mom and Dad and tell them where we are," he said. "But I don't think there's any other way we can reach them," he added glumly.

While Ben filled glasses with water from a pump at the sink, Lizzy showed Will and Annie where they could find jam, biscuits, crackers and bread in the cupboards, and cheese, milk and fruit in the icebox. There was smoked venison in a jar next to the stove. Spreading everything out on the large wooden table in the center of the room, they all pulled up chairs and began to eat. Their problems seemed distant for the time being. They had forgotten how hungry they were. And the light that brightened the space somehow gave them hope.

As they ate, Will and Annie looked around the room. There were no cartons of food, except for some cereal in boxes. For Ben and Lizzy, it appeared their food was kept in containers until it could be prepared for them. No frozen meals for them. Everything smelled and tasted fresh.

It was a world different from the one they knew. Annie couldn't hold back anymore. She blurted out the question that had been nagging at her.

"What year is it?"

"What do you mean, what year is it?" Ben said, with a touch of impatience. "That's a silly thing to ask."

"No, it's not. I think it may be important to know your answer. What year is it?"

Ben glanced at his sister, puzzled, and then he looked back at Annie.

"It's 1912."

Ben was serious. To him, it really was 1912. And when Will and Annie told him that for them, the year was 2021, he stared at them, eyes and mouth wide open, speechless. This was getting scary. If it was really 1912, there would be no way of reaching their parents. They wouldn't have been born yet.

It was hard for the four of them to believe they were from two different centuries. But how did it happen? It dawned on Will that he and Annie might have gone through a time warp of some kind. Was there any point in suggesting it? And trying to find a common ground in their two different sets of experiences was going to be hard. Some things wouldn't have any meaning for many years after the era Ben and Lizzy knew. Living in the early 20th century, they would be familiar with horseless carriages and automobiles and maybe even flying machines. But was there anything that would give them some understanding of the predicament Will was sure they were in?

On a hunch, Will asked Ben, "Have you ever heard of time travel?"

"Sure. Like in *The Time Machine*? That's one of my favorite books."

Annie and Will knew H.G. Wells' famous story only from an old movie they had seen on television. And Will had read lots of stories about time travel. The concept of something that transported people to another time turned out to be something they could all understand.

"I think that may be what happened to Annie and me," Will said.

"You're suggesting that you and Annie somehow stepped into some kind of time machine that brought you to the year 1912?" Ben asked.

"That's the basic idea, yes. Or maybe we didn't even have to step into a machine. We just fell into some other way of going back in time. Some sort of portal that we accidentally went through on this mountain."

"But if you are the ones who have traveled through time, what does it have to do with us? Is it connected to our father's disappearance?" Ben asked.

Will thought for a moment. "I don't know what happened to him. And I don't know why or how we ended up here with you. But if Annie and I really did travel back almost a hundred years—I mean, how can we return to our own time?"

Ben struggled to grasp what Will was describing. It was far beyond anything he had studied in school. Annie was beginning to have another idea.

"Maybe the house is the portal," she said. "Everything went crazy after we were here before and then saw it disappear."

"So DO you think we should get out of here?" Will asked. "Stock up with food and then try to find our way home in the morning?"

Lizzy looked at her brother. When she spoke, her voice was small and quiet. "Ben, if they go back to wherever they were, we'll be alone again. And I don't want to be alone. I want us to find Mommy and Daddy. Maybe they can help us."

Annie nodded and reached out to touch Lizzy on her shoulder. "You're right. We can't leave you here alone."

"If Father doesn't come back by tomorrow morning, we'll go with you," Ben said. "And if he does come back, he'll know what to do."

"That settles it," Will answered. We're in this together." He was glad they had a plan, but he could see it wouldn't be easy to fill their backpacks for their trip down the mountain because of the way the food was stored. There were no small packages or items like granola bars that would be easy to carry if they left the house. Everything was in sacks or loose in compartments in kitchen cupboards and drawers. Food that was easily portable was obviously waiting to be developed in a later era.

Will began gathering together some extra portions of everything they had eaten and squeezed them into his backpack. He stuffed a couple of the granola bars they had brought with them into his pockets. Annie followed suit. Ben found a straw basket in the corner of the room and brought it to the table where he filled it with the rest of the food. After they were satisfied that they had enough set aside. Will pulled out a piece of paper and a pencil from his coat pocket. Poised to start taking notes, he looked around at his companions.

"Let's see if we can make a list of everything we know about the mountain. Maybe it will point to some options we haven't considered. Let's start with the house."

"What about it?"

"Isn't it pretty modern for 1912? I mean, you have inside water. And electricity." With his interest in science, there were lots of things he wanted to know.

Ben nodded, his pride visible in his face. "Father wanted it to be the most up-to-date residence in this part of the United States."

"But how did he manage to design a home with so many modern features?"

"He built the last house we lived in. This place is a lot like that one."

"But I'll bet the other one wasn't built on a mountain. Where water was hard to find."

"It wasn't hard to find. That road that we followed up the other side of the ridge—that's how all the materials for building this house were brought up here. And there's a river that runs through the canyon down there. That's where Father's engineering came in. He knew how to use pumps and build the lines to bring the water up here. We have to be careful with it, but we have enough for cooking and other stuff."

"It must have been a big project," Will said, trying to imagine all that would have been required. "Did he build the mansion all by himself?"

"No. There were lots of skilled workmen in the valley who were available to help. But he designed everything and made sure it was done quickly. The house was built in less than a year."

"Amazing." It was the only word Annie could come up with. Ben beamed and Lizzy even managed a giggle. "Your father must be a genius."

"Yeah, probably.... He has some quirky traits, but he's always coming up with interesting stuff in his laboratory."

"Laboratory? Where's that?"

"In the basement. He spends a lot of time there."

"Can we see it?" Will was getting excited now.

Ben looked shocked. "Oh no. Father never lets us see the laboratory. We have never been there. Never."

"But he's not here now. He wouldn't know."

"That doesn't matter. If he comes back—I mean when he comes back—he'll be angry if he knows we got into his laboratory. No—just no. We won't go there."

ANNIE LOOKED at Will, eyebrows raised. Ben noticed and stood up abruptly, knocking his chair over.

"I know what you're thinking!" he flared. "That my father is some sort of mad scientist who is cooking up trouble in his laboratory. But he's not. He's just a smart guy who likes gadgets and tinkering with his projects. And he doesn't want us in the lab because we might get hurt on some of his contraptions, that's all!"

Will's response was just as sharp. Rising from his chair, fists clenched at his side, he struggled to keep his voice calm but firm. It was a side of her brother that Annie had never seen before. "If we accidentally enter the portal again and go back even farther in time, neither your father nor the laboratory will be around to help us," he shouted. "I have a sneaky feeling that we might find something in the lab that could show us how to get out of this mess. We need to see what's there."

Ben and Will stood nose to nose for a moment until Lizzy moved next to her brother and tugged at his sleeve. "Ben, if there's anything in that room that could help us, Daddy would want us to see it."

Ben turned and looked at Lizzy. His shoulders relaxed and his face softened. "You could be right," he said, calming down. "Maybe whatever he was doing in the laboratory does have something to do with what is going on here now. It might be our best hope."

H E ROSE and headed out of the kitchen back toward the library. "Follow me," he said, waving at the others. "I know where the key is."

The big door was unyielding until the two boys leaned against it with their shoulders and pushed. It opened with a loud squeak onto a stairway that led into darkness.

"I'm pretty sure there's a light here somewhere," Ben said, waving his hand above and in front of him until he found the string hanging from a lightbulb above his head. He tugged it, and the landing where the four of them stood was instantly bright. They moved cautiously down the stairs, arriving at a work area where another light hung from the low ceiling just above a work bench and some electrical equipment. Ben pulled the string that turned it on and stepped back so all of them could size up the room and the equipment that took up most of the space there. Electrical boxes—one with a dial and the other with a red button and a switch—were arranged neatly on the table next to the work bench. In the corner of the basement was a large closet-like enclosure whose door stood open. A buzzing sound came from it and a pale blue light flashed from within.

Ben walked over to the enclosure and peeked inside.

"Be careful!" Annie called out.

"I will. I just want to know what this is. It seems to have some sort of machine in it that is still running." He moved closer, studying the walls of the strange closet. "There's a seat in here. And lots of dials and switches. This is a place where you're supposed to sit down and do something."

"Or go somewhere," Will said, walking over to stand next to Ben. "You know what this reminds me of, Annie? The transporter in that movie we saw about time travel." He turned to Ben. "I think this might explain what happened to your father. Why he isn't anywhere around here right now. He may have been transported to another place using this contraption. But it's still running, so he may be planning to come back."

"But where would he go?" Ben asked, scratching his head.

Lizzy moved next to him and peeked inside the enclosure. She wasn't crying now. Just curious. "To find Mommy, Ben. That's where he would go. If this is where they are, I want to be there too." She stepped inside the opening.

"Lizzy don't!" Ben cried out and reached for her. As he grabbed her arm, the buzzing in the machine grew louder, and blue crackling beams shot out and expanded, drawing him into the machine after his sister.

Will and Annie watched horrified as Ben and Lizzy disappeared in a flash of light. The machine's buzzing grew louder and the basement began to rumble. Will grabbed Annie's hand. "We've got to get out of here, fast!"

They hurried up the stairs and raced through the kitchen, heading down the hallway. As they passed through the library, a loud ROARRR startled them. It was coming from the fireplace. The lion whose face decorated the top of the opening shook his mane and glared at them. He roared again. Will and Annie leaped back at the sound.

"He means business," Will said. "It's a good thing he's stuck in the stone."

On the other wall, the buck moved his head from side to side as if to break free. His sad brown eyes looked directly at Annie, pleading with her.

The house was alive. Literally.

"Annie, we have to keep moving," Will shouted. The house was shaking so hard, he and his sister had trouble keeping their balance. They started running again but Annie stumbled and fell. Will grabbed her arm and pulled her up, swaying and fighting against the back and forth motion of the walls surrounding them. "Just a few more steps, Annie! We have to make it!"

Staggering and careening out of the library and into the entry way, they threw open the front door and ran down the front steps. Just in time. With a rumble and a blinding blaze of light, the house disappeared again.

THE MYSTERY
OF THE MOUNTAIN

Lost and Alone

They stood, stunned, in the clearing where the house had been. The space seemed larger now, barren, lacking everything that had been there just moments before. Only the moss-covered boulder still lay to the side. Nothing was left but emptiness and silence. Their backpacks, with the food and supplies they held, had disappeared along with the house.

"So now you've done it," they heard a gruff and throaty voice say. They looked in its direction and saw something coming toward them out of the shadows of the forest—a wild animal, a beast of some kind, thin with shaggy fur, and eyes that shone. Its sharp front teeth poked out of a mouth that was twisted into a grimace. Slowly and stealthily, it crept their way until it stood directly in front of them. Teeth bared and head bowed, it looked up at them and growled. A musky smell filled the air around him.

"Oh my gosh, Will. It's some kind of wolf," Annie gasped.

"Get away from us," Will said, waving his arms to frighten the animal, his voice somewhere between a squeak and a squawk. He was trying to be brave for Annie, whose eyes and mouth were wide open. "Go back to the forest!"

"You dare to tell me what to do?" the animal snarled. "Those are our woods and this is our mountain. They have been since long before your kind came here and tried to crowd us out." His lips curled back even more, as his narrow eyes glinted at the children. And then, looking at Annie, his gaze softened.

"Others like you have done it one too many times," he said, his eyes filled with sadness. "Tested the magic of the mountain. And now your friends are gone, and you are at our mercy."

"That's not fair!" Annie said. "We didn't mean to be here!"

"That doesn't matter," the beast replied. "You're in our world now. And you may have to suffer for what others like you have done to us."

ANNIE PULLED herself up to her full height and took a step forward. Will grabbed her arm, holding her before she could move any farther. Pulling her arm loose, she stared hard at the wolf. "We don't want to be here," she said again, anger creeping into her voice. "All we want now is to get back to where we came from. To our own time and place. Some kind of portal brought us here. We'll find it again."

"The portal? Haven't you noticed that when you used it, you ended up being a long way from where you wanted to be?"

Annie looked back at Will, who nodded. He stared at the beast, looking defeated.

The animal, whatever he was, could sense their growing fear as what he was telling them began to sink in. He pranced around, glowering at them before he stopped to speak again. "The next time you use the portal, as you call it, everything you have known up until now will disappear completely and you will be alone on this mountaintop. Alone except for all of us. We'll see how clever you are then."

The beast turned and almost as an afterthought added, "unless I decide to help you." And then he loped away. Will and Annie watched. Neither one felt like talking. "When is this all going to end?" she said. "Are we ever going to get back home?"

And then they saw the other animals racing toward them, barking and howling, a small pack of scraggly creatures—four or five of them, teeth bared, eyes fixed on Annie and Will, ready to attack, waiting only for a signal. From the other side of the clearing, another pack of animals began closing in on them, padding stealthily across the open space in their direction.

Will grabbed Annie's arm and she followed as he started to run toward the edge of the forest. "We have to get out of here!" he cried. "Or they're going to kill us!"

The two sprinted toward the tree line, hoping to find cover there. Moving as fast as they could, they heard the animals coming after them. Annie looked over her shoulder and saw them, their mouths open, foaming.

"We can't outrun them, Will!" Annie called out, gasping.

"Look! Over there," he shouted, pointing at a tall, sprawling oak tree ahead of them. Massive, majestic, its roots reaching deep into the ground, its branches stretching upward toward the sun. A fortress. "The pack won't be able to catch us if we climb up there."

They stumbled over the mossy undergrowth between the smaller trees that stood in their way until Will reached the oak. Leaping up to grab a low-hanging branch, he scrambled onto it and then reached down and pulled Annie up alongside him.

"They'll follow us!" she shouted.

"No they won't! Just keep climbing!"

The two inched their way along the branch until they reached the massive trunk. Grabbing on tight, they hugged the rugged surface and pulled themselves upward until they were completely covered by leaves concealing them from the pack below. They were safe, out of reach of the beasts that had gathered at the base of the tree, yelping and bark-ing. With the two children hidden from their view, the pack began slinking away into the forest, still barking, until at last all was silent again except for Will and Annie's labored breathing.

"I think we're O.K.," Will said.

"For now, maybe," Annie said. "But we can't stay up here forever. If we get back on the ground, will they chase us again?"

"I'm not sure," he answered. "And if we do get back on the ground, where will we be? Near our cabin? If it's there again?"

They were protected from attack by the animals, but they seemed to be in another predicament that was even worse.

SUDDENLY ANNIE whispered. "Will, can you feel that? The trees are leaning toward each other."

And so they were. As the wind at the top of the canopy picked up, the branch on which they were perched swayed slowly, and bent toward the tall oak next to it, making it possible for Will and Annie to climb even higher. The upper branches of several trees were linked together. Will reached out with his hand and pulled on one of the larger limbs of the tree next to them. It seemed sturdy, a bridge strong enough to support his weight, so he and Annie crawled onto it.

Will looked back wide eyed at Annie. "We won't have to go back down to the ground yet," he said. "We can get away up here if we let the trees help us."

She hesitated. "Are you sure? This is just too weird. I don't trust it."

"Annie, it's our only hope. Either we take advantage of this or we're stuck here. Come on!"

Slowly, glancing fearfully at the ground far below, Annie followed her brother through a web of interlocking limbs and branches until they reached a point where they could see the rocky ground opening into a clearing below.

He looked out over the treetops. Barely visible in the distance was the canyon Ben had told them about. "I don't think we want to keep going this way," he said. "I can see the canyon on the other side of the mountain." He turned around and pointed in the opposite direction. "I think our cabin should be over there." He paused. "I can't see it there." He was feeling desperate, but he didn't want to scare Annie. He looked down at the forest floor and tried to sound hopeful. "This looks safe," he said. "We lost the pack."

"Isn't this where the deer were headed when we came down the mountain?" Annie said.

W ILL PEERED down through the leaves. "I can't tell. If you're right, that might be good. We should be able to find our way home from that spot."

"Are you sure? We almost got lost the last time we were there."

"We don't have any choice!" Will was losing patience with her. She was usually more willing to take chances than he. It wasn't like her to be so cautious. "The canopy stops here," he said. "Either we climb down and try to find our way out or we're stuck up here. We need to do something now. It's getting dark and we have to find someplace safe."

They climbed down the trunk of the tree. Will went first, testing the strength of the branches as he descended, Annie following. They lowered themselves from limb to limb until finally they were close enough to drop out onto the ground. Brushing bits of leaves and moss off their clothes, they looked around to get their bearings. Ahead of them was a grove of aspen trees swaying in the gentle wind that was blowing toward them. And between the trees, looking at them, they saw the deer again, four this time. A doe, two fawns and a buck with a huge rack of antlers.

"Will!" Annie whispered. "It looks like the same deer who have been following us."

"I think you're right," he answered. "Except the buck. We haven't seen him before, have we?" The buck looked at Will, his eyes flickering. And then the animals began moving away, through the aspens. They stopped once and glanced back at Will and Annie.

"They seem to want us to follow them," Annie said. "And I think we should this time."

Another World

The terrain was rocky, broken only by a thick undergrowth of ferns and sagebrush. They were leaving the forest, entering a lower elevation, but it took more effort than their other trips on the mountain. Where were the deer leading them? They saw the animals disappear, swallowed up by a large hole in a huge rock formation that blocked the trail they were taking. Annie and Will hesitated.

"We need to be careful about following them into that cave," Annie said, staring at the opening. "If they bolt, they could knock us down."

"But they meant to bring us here," Will said. "I'm convinced of that. Remember our dream? The fawns asked us to help them. I think this is where they want us to come for some reason."

CAREFULLY, he approached the opening, peered inside and motioned to Annie. "Come here," he said as he stared into the cave. "I can see some sort of light." Annie drew close to her brother and looked at the glow that brightened the space just inside the opening in the rocks. It wasn't sunlight. Too late in the day for that. It was more like a beam shining through a gradually opening door or window. Suddenly they felt the tingling sensation again—the one they had felt earlier in the fireplace at the old house. This time it was stronger, and it drew them toward the lighted entrance of the cave.

At first, there was only the sound of briskly rustling branches, but that quickly became a loud whoosh and then a roar. The beam began to lengthen and extend, enveloping them, stretching out and carrying them toward a vanishing point. Their hearts were pounding, and their heads spinning.

And then they passed out.

The next thing they knew, they were in a giant underground cavern, lying at the edge of a murky pool fed by water trickling down from high above them, dripping over the soft, lumpy surface of the surrounding wall. Annie sat up, lightheaded from their trip through the beam of light. She grasped her forehead with both hands. "Cobwebs," she muttered. "My head feels like cobwebs." She couldn't tell if she was still asleep, or half awake.

Will rubbed his eyes and rose gradually to a kneeling position so he could get a better look at where they were. The area around the pool was filled with gaps and crevices. A few were large enough that they looked like they were tunnels leading farther into the cave. A thick layer of moss covered the ledge behind the pool. The whole place smelled of rotting vegetation.

Will sneezed and wiped his nose. Annie peered into the darkness of the space behind them. All she could see was the opening to a dimly lit narrow passage.

"How did we get here?" she asked Will. "Do you remember anything?"

"Not really," Will said. "We were outside the cave and all of a sudden we're here. There was a light...but it's all very fuzzy to me now."

"It's the same for me." Annie's brow was furrowed, as she thought hard, trying to make sense of the strange situation they were in.

Still kneeling, they looked around. In the semi-darkness, they glimpsed a slippery narrow path alongside the pond that seemed to lead into a large gap behind. "Should we head that way?" Annie asked, pointing. "We don't remember how we got into this place, so we don't really know how to get out."

They looked around again. The walls on all sides had no other crevices wide enough to provide an escape.

"The big hole behind the pond might be the only way out." Will said. "Let's go there." He got up and stood as straight and tall as he could. Annie scrambled to her feet after him and together the two moved toward the opening.

The surface inside it was squishy and soft, but they kept their balance by steadying themselves against the surrounding walls. Inching their way along, they entered another wide space with high, looming walls.

"Welcome. We've been waiting for you," a voice announced, startling them. They stopped and looked in the direction of the sound. They tried to focus their eyes on the shadowy presence emerging from the side of the cave, but it was hard to see anything very clearly. Light coming from high above them was no more than a faint glimmer on the cavern floor.

"Who's there?" Will said, squinting and straining to see the source of the voice. Annie moved closer to her brother, peering at the approaching form.

I⊤ WAS a buck with huge antlers, partly obscured in a shimmering mist. Annie and Will held their hands in front of their eyes to shield them from the light, which became even brighter as the animal came closer. By the time it stood a couple of feet away, the intensity of the glare made their heads hurt. A billowy cloud filled with sparkling beams spitting out flashes of some kind of electricity descended on them. Within it, the buck transformed into a ghostlike human figure whose outlines were barely visible. It reached out a hand and waved it slowly.

"I'm sorry," it said. "I didn't mean to frighten you."

[84]

The glow faded away and Annie and Will's headaches disappeared. Standing in front of them was a man dressed in slacks and an old-fashioned sweater.

"W-w-who are you?" Will stammered.

"My name is Elliott," the man said. "I believe you have met my children."

"Your children?" Will asked in a shaky voice. "What are you talking about?"

"Ben and Lizzy."

Annie shuddered. *Were Ben and Lizzy ghosts too?*

"Don't be afraid," Elliott said, in a voice that was thin and scratchy, sort of like the static that Annie and Will had heard on distant stations on the car radio. While he spoke, the doe and her two fawns reappeared behind him.

"Follow them," Elliott said again, louder with more urgency. "If you help us, we can help you."

As if in a dream, Annie and Will moved toward the three deer, who resumed their pace on the mossy ridge and headed into the darker depths of the cave. The two children walked slowly, trying not to lose their footing on the slippery path. The deer by now had disappeared through a crevice in the back wall. A dim light beckoned from whatever lay beyond and lit the trail that Annie and Will continued to follow, stepping carefully through the sticky debris that lay in their way.

When they passed through the gap, they stopped. They weren't in the cave anymore. They had entered an area that looked a lot like the library in the house on top of the mountain, although not exactly. A huge fireplace dominated the far end of the room, but there were no bookcases lining the other walls. And the deer weren't there either.

A woman in an old-fashioned dress and lace collar ringing her neckline smiled at them. Next to her was the man who had called himself Elliot, in his sweater and slacks. And in front of both in the strange old clothes they were wearing when they first met Will and Annie were Ben and Lizzy, who smiled and clapped their hands, happy to see their friends again.

"Are you the deer?" Annie exclaimed. Their constant and mysterious presence on the mountain had fascinated her, and now she understood who they were.

Elliott nodded. "We've been trying to lead you here."

"How? And why are you deer?"

"Because that's the only way we can move around in your time and your world. Otherwise we're trapped in this cave. We need your help."

It was hard to believe what he was saying. But nothing else could explain the strange experiences they had been having.

Lizzy ran toward them and wrapped her arms around Annie's waist. Ben walked up to Will and extended his hand in greeting. "I knew you would be the ones to help us," Ben said.

"Help you? How?"

"Help us break the spell that keeps us here."

What Spell?

"Spell? What are you talking about?" Will was nervous but curious too. His voice was shaky. He looked around the room. "What is this place?"

The woman walked quickly over to Annie and Will and knelt to hug each of them. She looked at Elliott and spoke, her tone deliberately quiet and calming. "Elliott, we're scaring them." She stood up and took both Will and Annie by the hand, leading them over to a dark brown sofa with carved wood arms and legs, part of an arrangement of furniture in the center of the room. There were tatted doilies on a table in front of the sofa. "You're probably tired, aren't you?" she asked gently.

Annie, for one of the few times in her life, was unable to speak. She nodded and sat down close to Will on the sofa. Lizzy and Ben took their places on the couch opposite them. "You're right, Elaine," Elliott said as he settled onto one of the two matching armchairs positioned at the side of the sofa. Elaine sat in the chair next to him.

Leaning forward, his arms on his knees, he looked intently at Annie and Will. "I've just begun to sort things out myself," he said. He hesitated, not sure how to explain something so complicated to youngsters not much older than his own children. "It's a little hard to describe because it's not the kind of spell you usually think of, where things change from one thing into another and stay that way. This is more of a flow back and forth. Between different worlds. For a while you are doing regular things and then all of a sudden, you're in another reality that is very strange and mystical. And then just as suddenly you're back to what you thought was your normal life."

Annie and Will were confused, but Will, with his interest in science, was full of questions. "What do you mean another reality? What's it like?"

[87]

"It's just animals and the forest on the mountain. No humans. No houses or towns nearby. And sometimes we're animals too. There's no pattern. It just happens."

Will needed to know more. "When did it all start?"

Elliott scratched his chin. "I think it began with an accident in my laboratory at our home out east." He reached out to Elaine and grasped her hand, squeezing it. "She was helping me with an experiment I was doing with electricity. Something went wrong and apparently she was transported to another dimension. That's what I at last suspected at the time. It turns out I was right about that."

"Why did she end up here?" Will asked. He was fascinated now by Elliott's story even though it still didn't make any sense to him.

"I'm not sure why," Elliott admitted. "I'm guessing that the flow between realities is between times or places related to each other. Elaine grew up in the town in the valley below. When she was young, she spent a lot of time exploring and hiking on this mountain. Being transported here was coming to a place in her memory."

"So did you find her when you built the house on the mountaintop?" Annie asked.

Elliott shook his head. "Not at first," he admitted. "But from the first times I came hiking on the mountain, I knew she was here. That's why I built the house on the ridge. To be close to that feeling."

"That is so…unbelievable," Annie blurted, unable to control her reaction. Will winced. Annie was being blunt again. She couldn't help herself. He could tell she was full of questions.

Elaine had been listening quietly to Elliott, but Annie's comment made her break her silence. "I know it sounds strange. But I wasn't aware of anything different. I was just young again, moving among the animals I loved so much. Especially the deer. They have always been my favorites. They let me move with them on the mountain and made me feel safe. It didn't feel like I was in that world very long. I even felt Elliott with me a couple of times."

Elliott joined in. "It was the same with Ben and Lizzy and me. We didn't notice anything unusual either. We were just living in our new house but also spending time in the town in the valley. We weren't aware of any other reality. Not until recently."

"What happened?" Will asked.

"I think it was because of the machine and the other equipment in my laboratory...the stuff that caused the accident with Elaine. I brought all of it with me from Ohio and kept it turned on. I believed it would help her find her way back to us." He looked at Elaine. "I got to thinking about the other dimension and I was sure I would find her there. So a couple of days ago, I stepped into the machine. I lost consciousness and woke up here, with Elaine. And then all of a sudden Ben and Lizzy were here too."

"This is where we came after we were with you in Father's laboratory," Ben said. He was excited to share his part of the story. "It was a really strange sensation. But when we woke up, we were so glad to be with mother again." Lizzy nodded happily. It was the first time Annie and Will had seen her smile so broadly.

NOBODY SPOKE. After what seemed like a very long silence, Annie looked around the room with its old-fashioned furniture and the huge fireplace. "So where are we now?"

"This is the library of our house back east. We're here because...well I think it's because...it's a memory shared by all of us.

Another question kept nagging at Annie. "Now that you're all together again, why don't you just leave this place and go back to your home on the mountaintop—or back to Ohio?"

"We can't," Elliott answered. "We already tried. When we go outside, we become part of a world of animals in another time and reality. There are good ones, we've found. Like the other deer. And the trees are alive too, in ways we hadn't realized before. But there's one creature that rules everything in that world—some kind of wolf. He seems to have us trapped here."

Another long pause. Elaine stood up abruptly. "That's enough, Elliott. This is hard for all of us to understand, and it's especially hard for Ben and Lizzy's friends."

Will was very quiet, still trying to figure out the biggest thing about Elliott's story that he didn't understand. "If it was the machine in your laboratory that transported you here," he asked, his brow wrinkled in thought, "how did Annie and I travel back in time? Or beam into this cave? We didn't enter the machine. There must be other ways to be transported. Other portals."

Elliott shook his head. "Things that can be explained by science are the only ones that make sense to me. The machine and the laboratory equipment transported the four of us here, into this world. I think I know how that works. Maybe they also turned the house into a portal for you. Maybe its all just a strange accident. But why we can't get out of this dimension and why we seem to go back and forth between different realities?" He paused.

Lizzy waved her hand at her father to get his attention.

"I think I know, Daddy. It's magic!"

$\mathcal{E}$LLIOTT SMILED, the love for his daughter showing in his face. "That may be the only explanation," he said softly. But as he reached out to pick her up, his image began to break up again. He gasped as he saw Elaine, Ben and Lizzy fade into the same billowy cloud filled with sparkling beams and flashes of electricity that Annie and Will had seen earlier. Before Elliott also disappeared into the glow of the cloud, he called out, his voice thin and staticky again. "Follow the tunnel. That's your only way…."

And then he was gone. So was the room where he and his family had been. Annie and Will found themselves sitting by themselves on a rock in the middle of a large cavern, with ledges reaching high above them. At the back of the cavern was a dark, narrow hole. Will pointed at it. "That must be the tunnel."

Annie lowered her head and stayed crouched on the rock. "I don't like caves. Especially this one. It's just too closed in and scary."

"We'll just have to trust what Elliott was trying to tell us," Will said, standing up and helping Annie get to her feet. Together, the two walked slowly toward the opening.

How Can We Get Out of Here?

The tunnel was narrow, in some places only wide enough for Annie and Will to squeeze through one at a time. Will went first, to find what lay ahead, and to reassure Annie that the passage was safe. He kept talking as he walked. At one time they both had to get on their knees and crawl beneath the low-ceilinged stone walls. After what seemed forever, the tunnel began to widen, leading into another cavern like the one where they had found Elliott and his family. But there was no homelike setting there. Just high ledges and outcroppings where small rodent-like creatures had built their nests, and a large dirt floor in the middle.

"What was that?" Annie asked as something flew overhead, chirping. Will could tell it was a bat, but he didn't answer. Where there was one, there would be more, and Annie would freak out if she knew what was in the air above her.

"Let's keep going," he mumbled, moving steadily on a path on the side of the cavern that led upward. "I think it's getting easier," he said, turning around to make sure Annie was following him closely. The next tight passage they squeezed through opened into an even larger space, filled with tapered accretions whose pointed tips rose from the floor, almost touching similar formations hanging down from the ceiling.

"What are those things?" Annie asked as she gazed at the forest of stone.

"Stalagmites and stalactites," Will answered, his voice filled with awe. "I read about them in a book I got at the library last year." They watched as the columns began to swing to and fro, twisting slowly and ominously toward them.

"We need to keep moving!" Will shouted. It seemed to be growing colder and colder. He and Annie darted out of the way of the threatening pillars and hurried toward the upward path. After struggling through another crevice, they entered another large cavern with walls that curved majestically together, toward a rocky roof high above them. Water trickled down the face of one of the walls into a small pool at its base. The animal life that had been so obvious in the first part of their hike wasn't visible here, and both began to relax, especially when a hint of light seeped into their surroundings.

T HIS PART of the cave was wide and open, its top seemingly supported by graceful arches of red stone. At the far end, rocky columns bent toward each other framing an entry that was a window opening onto a broad expanse of trees and undergrowth.

"We're almost outside!" Will yelled. The words were barely out of his mouth before the walls began to shake, the columns began to lean dangerously inward, and a rumble could be heard coming from deep within the cave behind them. They raced through the opening and flung themselves on the grassy undergrowth beneath a stand of small trees.

They looked back and saw the entry to the cave close and vanish into the solid face of a rocky hillside.

Annie scrambled over to Will. "Wh...what just happened?"

"I don't know. But we need to get away from here."

The two rose to their feet and tried to figure out where they were. They wanted to find their way home, but without the compass that had been in Will's lost backpack, they couldn't be sure which direction might lead them to their cabin, if it was there. "I think it's that way," he said, pointing across the mountain. "Let's go before it gets too dark."

The two of them held hands as they moved slowly through the undergrowth and the rugged trail toward a grove of larger trees. Finally they found their way to a path just below the woods. A familiar roof loomed in the distance. "I can see our cabin again!" Will shouted and Annie cheered. Scrambling over the rocks and through the thick grass, it would be only a few minutes before they were home.

They weren't prepared for what they found. The furnishings inside the cabin were entirely different than they had been. There was no couch where their father had sat reading. Instead, there were three ancient, overstuffed chairs arranged around a thick log coffee table. The kitchen area was also sparsely decorated. The table where they had eaten breakfast was gone, and in its place was a rickety picnic table, with attached benches. Gone, too, were all of the dishes and the food their parents had brought with them for the vacation.

Will and Annie ran down the hall to the other rooms, but they found no evidence of their parents. The decor was minimal, just a couple of beds and small wooden chests of drawers. The cabin was largely vacant and dusty, ready perhaps for the next group of occupants to bring it back to life.

Annie was truly frightened. She turned to her brother. "Where are Mom and Dad?"

Will had withdrawn into his own thoughts. He was staring at the floor, so quiet Annie wasn't sure for a minute that he had heard her. When he spoke it was almost a whisper.

"I don't know. They're just gone. I think we may have entered into another time—later than Elliott and his family, but not when our parents are alive."

"What are we going to do? Do you think maybe we can find a neighbor who can help us?" Annie asked.

"No one lives close by. I remember that was what Dad liked about this place when he rented it." Will said glumly. "These stupid cabins are set so far apart, we'd have to walk quite a ways to find anybody."

"Do you suppose they are all missing too?" Annie asked.

"I don't know." Will was searching for a logical response. "If we could find a car, we could drive to town."

"You're not old enough to drive. What if we got stopped along the way?" she said.

"That would be O.K. If we found anybody who could help us that way, we could have them bring us back to show them what is going on here. Or get them to take us someplace to find help. And if we got all the way to town without being stopped, we could go right to the police station."

"Are you sure you would know how to drive on these mountain roads?" Annie asked.

W ILL HESITATED. It wasn't that he didn't know how to drive—he did, sort of. Their father occasionally allowed him to drive the family car in the empty areas of the big parking lot next to the shopping center in their hometown on weekend mornings before the mall opened. "You'll have to learn sometime," their father had said. "Best to practice when I am in the car and can give you pointers." But that was driving on a flat surface with no other cars around. Will was tall enough to reach the gas pedal and see over the steering wheel, but he had never practiced driving on an actual road—and certainly not one that was steep and winding, in the dark.

"I could probably do it," he said, but the depth of their dilemma was becoming clear. "That's beside the point. We don't have keys to any car we might find."

"What about bikes or something like that?' Annie asked "We can't sit here and do nothing. We have to find someone who can help us. Let's check the garage at the bottom of the walk."

What they they found wasn't a surprise. There was no sign that any vehicle had been parked there recently. Nor were there any bicycles or other way of getting around.

They were stranded. Neither of them could think of anything to say. Annie finally broke the silence. "So how are we going to get out of this mess?" she asked. Fear was setting in. The situation seemed hopeless.

"I think there is no point in trying to find anybody else," Will said quietly. "I've been thinking. If we did find someone, the reality is that they would be living in this time, not the time we want to get back to. We'd be stuck here.

"If this is reality," Annie said, her voice shaky and thin, "then reality sucks."

Will reached out and pulled his sister to him. They clung tightly to each other for several minutes. Both were shivering.

F INALLY, they went back to the deck and sat on the chairs they found there. They gazed morosely at the view that had once seemed so pleasant and restful and now seemed so strange and foreboding,

After a long period of silence, Annie spoke, this time in the matter-of-fact tone that she always adopted when she was concentrating on a problem. "We should start by trying to figure out why we are here and why we are the only ones who are left. What kept us from disappearing along with Elliott and his family and now Mom and Dad? And how can we reverse what happened to us?"

She paused and turned to look at her brother.

Will thought for a while and nodded. "Well, if everything started with our going to the old mansion, maybe the only way to change things is to hike back up the mountain again. Maybe that's how to get things back to the way they should be. It probably matters if we do everything exactly the way we did before," he said.

Annie was impatient. "Why bother? We know we just need to get up there. I don't care how we do it."

"No Annie. We have to be careful how we do it. Remember that movie we saw last year about time travel? The people got back to their own time by retracing their steps."

It wasn't something that either one of them wanted to do. But they were pretty sure they had no choice. So the went back into the cabin, and began to make preparations for another trek up the mountain.

It was too late at night for them to leave immediately. They would have to wait until morning. Sitting at the picnic table in the breakfast area, the light of the full moon outside coming through the window, Will began by making step by step plans for their return up the mountain. He started with a map of the route they should take, to be sure it was the exact path they had followed when they found the house at the top of the mountain. Plans compete, they curled up on two of the overstuffed chairs in the area next to the kitchen and fell into a fitful sleep.

They awoke early to sun beams seeping through the curtains in the windows overlooking the deck outside. There was no food in the cabin, but they still had the granola bars in their pockets left over from the stocking up they did with Ben and Lizzy. After a quick snack, they were ready to leave. They checked once more to see if their parents were outside the cabin, or anywhere else on the property where they might have missed them before. Nothing had changed. They were still alone.

How It Should Be

Guided by the light of the awakening day, they followed the trail that led up to the top of the mountain. As they walked, Annie stopped and pointed to the varieties of plant life that surrounded them. Gambel oak mainly. And some young pine trees and aspen. "I don't think these are the trees we've seen before. They look different. Everything looks different."

They kept walking and found themselves once again where the mansion used to be. There, perched on the moss-covered boulder in the middle of the clearing, was the wolf-beast staring at them, his gaze less threatening now. At the sides of the clearing other animals—deer, foxes, rabbits and some other smaller creatures—stood watching.

"This is the way the mountain was before it was spoiled," the wolf said. He hopped down from the boulder and moved toward them, the musky wet fur smell growing stronger as he approached.

"Spoiled? How? We didn't do anything to it," Annie protested.

W̷ILL WAS relieved. Frightened as she had been the night before, Annie was her blunt and mouthy self again.

"Not you," the wolf-beast responded. "Others like you. The ones that built the house here on the mountain. They cut down trees, tore up the undergrowth, opened ways to bring supplies they needed, dug channels that didn't exist before to carry water where it wasn't supposed to flow—and killed some of us."

Will sighed. "He means the house that Elliott and the workmen built. The roads, the plumbing, and the materials they used for construction. They would have changed the mountain, that's for sure."

"Changed? Ruined!" the wolf growled. "There's only one way we can stop it from getting worse. Restoring our world. Returning things to the way they were before. Protecting it."

Will scratched his head. He and Annie were caught in a condition that couldn't be explained by any science he had learned in school or read about in any books. It sounded more like Elliott's description of reality flowing back and forth. But something didn't add up. "Whenever you return things to the way they were," he said to the wolf, "they don't always stay there, do they?"

The beast shook his head from side to side. "No," he said,"the pull of the other realities is very strong. But we have a stronger force. Our, what you call, magic."

"That won't restore things forever," Will said. "Magic didn't make the house or the changes on the mountain go away completely. When we were in the house as it started to disappear, we were sent to an earlier time. But we're still on the mountain. And so are Elliott and his family."

"I do what I have to do to protect the mountain." the beast replied firmly. "And I will keep doing it. This is sacred space. Ours."

ANNIE LOOKED directly at him. Something had just occurred to her. "You talk to us, but not to the others. And you have not trapped us, like you did Elliott and his family. Why?"

The beast stared back at her, his gaze so intense it felt like it was burning into her. He settled on his haunches.

[100]

"I have been following you. I have seen how you love animals. I brought you here. Because I sense you understand," he answered in a gruff but soft growl. "You can help us."

There was a long silence. Will looked over at Annie. She continued to study the beast. She did understand. And she felt sorrow for the animal, for them all. His world—the world of the forest and the animals who lived there—had truly been disrupted by humans living on the mountain. But maybe tha didn't have to happen. She thought hard for a moment, and then her face brightened.

"I have an idea!" she exclaimed. "Instead of trying to return the mountain to the way it was before, why not just send the people who changed it back to whatever they were before?"

Will was surprised. Annie's idea was pretty logical and scientific—for her. Maybe even workable? Would the beast agree? How would he do it?

"LET THEM remember?" she asked.

The beast's answer came right away. The beast raised up on his hind legs, pointed his head to the sky, his form growing larger and larger until it was so big it blocked the moon. He dropped down to his four paws and looked first at Will. Then he stared at Annie for what seemed like a very long time, although it was probably only a minute or two. He was regarding her with curiosity and something more. Acceptance. Maybe even kindness. He bared his teeth and twisted his lips into something that looked very much like a smile. "Don't forget what you have learned," he growled. Dipping his head, he turned and raced into the forest, disappearing in the mist. The other animals who had been watching followed him.

The children felt a billowing cloud close in around them. And then they fell asleep.

When they woke up, they were sitting in the chairs on the deck of their cabin, stacks of books piled next to them. Will rubbed his eyes and yawned. "I guess we fell asleep," he said. He looked down and noticed some moss stuck in his shirt sleeve. He pulled it out and stared at it. "Where did this come from?"

"We were pretty tired after our trip here yesterday," Annie said, stretching. She leaned over to start picking up the books that were at her feet.

Their father was coming up the path leading to their cabin, carrying a couple of bags of groceries. "What do you kids feel like doing today?" he asked as he walked up the stairs onto the deck.

"MAYBE GO for a hike up the mountain?" Annie suggested, looking up the slope behind their cabin.

"That's federal land," he answered. "An area where the wilderness is protected. Has been for a long time. At least that's what the guy at the grocery store told me." He adjusted the bags he was carrying as he headed for the front door of the cabin. "It might be interesting but I'm not sure how much we could see up there. How about if we go fishing instead? There's a pond stocked with fish on the edge of town, and I'll bet we can rent some rods there. We can go after lunch."

Annie shook her head. "I don't want to kill any fish," she said. She knew she needed to be respectful of the lives of other living creatures but she couldn't remember why.

"Don't worry," her father answered with a chuckle. "It's

a catch and release pond. The fish will be O.K." He paused an shifted the bags he was carrying. "But I have another idea. Before we go fishing, let's stop by the electronics store in the town in the valley. We can buy that cell phone that Will keeps saying he wants for his birthday."

Will leaped out of his chair and pumped his arms. "That would be awesome!" he exclaimed, ready to head into town.

Annie gathered up their books and followed him into the cabin.

*****

T HE LOUD pop and flash of light from Elliott's basement laboratory startled everyone in the Hansinger household. Ben and Lizzy were upstairs in their bedrooms. Their mother was tucking Lizzy into bed for the night. "Oh, for heaven's sake," Elaine said. "Not again!" Exasperated, she hurried downstairs. "Elliott," she shouted, "stop whatever you're doing. You're frightening the children!" She paused to catch her breath. "And that old busybody, Bertha Hemingway, is probably going to call Bill Gerhardt out here again!"

Elliott's voice could barely be heard as he came slowly up the basement stairs. "No need to worry, Elaine." Entering the kitchen, he brushed some debris off his sweater. "I think the machine is broken for good now," he said. He looked dejected. "I can't get it to work anymore. I'll have to come up with another experiment."

"You're too preoccupied with those contraptions. Will you stop now?" she demanded. "The children need you to spend more time with them."

Elliott closed the door to the basement behind him and walked over to Elaine. He wrapped his arms around her waist. "You're right," he said, kissing her on the forehead. "Starting tomorrow that's exactly what I'll do."

*****

THE WOLF-BEAST ambles through the woods, content with what he sees. He is young and healthy, not old and scraggly. So is the forest. The trees are not yet as tall, but their roots are already intertwined, a hidden community. Songbirds flit and nest in their branches, watchful of the hawks and other predators that can swoop down after them. Everywhere, creatures thrive even when they are sometimes at risk. There is an order to life in the forest—nature's order, not one imposed by human intervention and design.

HE IS their protector, guardian of all that exists on the mountain. Pausing to survey his domain, he is satisfied:

My work is done for now. I can rest. But I will return again if necessary.

He trots up to the ridge of the mountain and looks around. Wind ruffles his fur while gusts buffet the rocks along the rugged crest. He tips his head back, points his snout toward the sky and howls, a long wail that ends in a growl. He looks around one more time before he returns to the wooded area below the summit. Just beyond the tree line, he disappears.

Made in the USA
Las Vegas, NV
12 July 2023